Whodunit Season 2 Live!

Alexis Jones

Published by Alexis Jones, 2024.

This is a work of fiction. Similarities to real people, places, or events are entirely coincidental.

WHODUNIT SEASON 2 LIVE!

First edition. October 21, 2024.

Copyright © 2024 Alexis Jones.

ISBN: 979-8224148868

Written by Alexis Jones.

The Northshore Academy of Martial Arts Dojo crew. You were there when I was younger and I don't know if I would be at the place I'm at now. You guys have been my rock in the past and I love the dojo. Thank you for being there for me when I was younger and being there for me now.

Alexandru Jociva, Thank you for being a great sensei and always believing in me. If it weren't for you, I don't know if this would be possible. You have helped me through so much and continue to be there for me.

Matthew Hibbeler, Thank you for being there when I need you. We may have our ups and downs, but there is always something between us that is unbreakable. These past few years have been wonderful and I love being with you. Thank you for helping me with this book, and many more to come. There is always going to be us, and I appreciate everything you have done. I love you so much and I don't know where I would be without you.

Season 2, Episode 1

As the curtain rises, we find ourselves enveloped in the opulent atmosphere of Langley Manor, a majestic estate steeped in history and mystery. A storm rages outside, but inside, guests mingle under the glow of chandeliers, their laughter mingling with the crackle of the fireplace. An air of anticipation hangs over the gathering, a mix of excitement and underlying tension.

Main Characters:

Alex Carter, the sharp eyed detective, surveys the scene, taking in the subtle dynamics of the guests with a blend of curiosity and caution. They exude an air of authority, ready to delve into the mysteries hidden among the attendees.

Victoria Langley, the enigmatic heiress, floats through the crowd, her elegant demeanor masking the turmoil brewing within. She glances at her family portraits on the walls, each one holding secrets of its own, her longing for freedom evident in her subtle movements.

Jordan Price, the skeptical observer, leans against a wall, arms crossed, rolling their eyes at the pretense of the event. Their sharp wit is matched only by their suspicion of the motives of those around them, ready to challenge the status quo.

Liam Torres, the charming rival, engages in light banter with the guests, his smile concealing a deeper ambition. He glances at Victoria with a mix of admiration and rivalry, aware that the stakes are higher than mere socializing.

Riley Brooks, the comic relief, bounces through the crowd with boundless energy, cracking jokes and trying to lighten the mood. They serve as the social glue, yet their playful facade hides a keen intelligence ready to uncover hidden truths.

ALEXIS JONES

As the evening unfolds, the storm outside intensifies, and the tension within the manor rises. Secrets lurk in every corner, and the stage is set for a night of intrigue, deception, and, inevitably, murder.

The curtain rises on a mystery waiting to unfold, a puzzle to be pieced together, and a gathering of individuals harboring dark truths. Welcome to Season 2 of Whodunit Live!

Act 1: The Murder

As the evening progresses, the atmosphere in Langley Manor becomes increasingly charged. Just as laughter fills the air, a sudden uproar disrupts the festivities. Gasps echo through the hall as Jordan Price collapses onto the marble floor, clutching their chest. Chaos erupts as guests rush to help, but it becomes clear—Jordan is dead, a victim of a sudden and mysterious affliction. Alex Carter springs into action, securing the area and initiating the investigation. The audience is invited to join them, questioning witnesses, examining evidence, and unraveling the tangled web of motives and secrets surrounding Jordan's untimely demise.

Act 2: The Investigation

As Detective Carter delves deeper into the investigation, a complex web of deceit and betrayal emerges, stretching far beyond the confines of Langley Manor. Suspects materialize, each harboring their motives and alibis, as the audience partners with Alex to sift through conflicting testimonies and hidden agendas.

Red herrings abound, and the tension escalates as secrets are unearthed. Each character reveals more than they intend, muddying the waters and leaving the audience guessing at every turn. Yet, amidst the chaos, one truth remains clear: someone in the room is responsible for Jordan's death, and it's up to the audience to unveil the culprit.

Option 1: Read the Interviews
Option 2: Accuse Victoria
Option 3: Accuse Liam
Option 4: Accuse Riley
Option 5: Accuse Alex
Option 6: Accuse a Hidden Guest

Whodunit "Live" Your Thoughts

This is where you can write your thoughts about who you think killed Jordan. You can do this before making your decision or after. There are plenty of moments throughout to make your choice.

Option 1: The Interviews

Victoria Langley

Alex: "Victoria, can you tell me about your relationship with Jordan?"

Victoria: (pausing, looking conflicted) "We had our differences. Jordan often challenged my decisions about the estate. They believed I was too protective of it."

Alex: "Did you notice anything unusual about Jordan tonight?"

Victoria: "Just their nervousness. They kept looking around like they were waiting for someone. I thought it was odd but didn't think much of it."

Alex: "Did you see anyone approach them before... before they collapsed?"

Victoria: (shakes her head) "No, I didn't. I was mingling with guests when it happened. But I wish I had paid closer attention."

Liam Torres

Alex: "Liam, you were close to Jordan. What do you think led to their death?"

Liam: (leaning back, a smirk playing on his lips) "Close? We had a business relationship, that's all. They could be insufferable, always pushing their agenda."

Alex: "Did you see anything suspicious before it happened?"

Liam: "I was in the study preparing for my speech. It's a good alibi, right? Besides, Jordan often overreacted. This could just be a dramatic stunt."

Alex: "And yet you don't seem too upset by it."

Liam: (shrugging) "I didn't like Jordan, but I didn't want them dead. I swear, I'm not a killer. I just want to keep my business safe."

Riley Brooks

Alex: "Riley, how do you feel about what happened to Jordan?"

Riley: (visibly shaken) "It's awful! I can't believe they're gone. I was just talking to them earlier, and they seemed... stressed."

Alex: "What were they stressed about?"

Riley: "They mentioned discovering something about the family's past. Something big. I didn't think much of it until now."

Alex: "Did you see anyone approach Jordan right before they collapsed?"

Riley: "I saw them talking to Victoria. They seemed tense. I thought maybe they were arguing."

Detective Alex Carter

Alex: (speaking aloud) "I need to analyze all the pieces. Who benefits from Jordan's death? Who had the opportunity?"

Thought Process: "Victoria may have felt threatened by Jordan's agenda. Liam has his ambitions. And Riley might know more than they let on about what Jordan discovered."

Conclusion: "I need to dig deeper into their relationships and see if there are any underlying motives that could lead to a murder."

If you have read the interviews and would like to write your thoughts, please return to page 3 to write your thoughts and your guess on Whodunit. After completing this, if you choose to, please return to acts 1 & 2 to review your options.

Option 2: Accuse Victoria

If you chose Victoria, you'd be correct! After Detective Alex asked her the first question, Victoria was visibly nervous. Below is a closer look at their relationship. Victoria, as the matriarch, was deeply invested in managing the family estate. Jordan, on the other hand, sought to assert their own vision or changes regarding the estate, often putting them at odds with Victoria. Jordan's willingness to question Victoria's decisions and seek transparency about the estate's operations created significant friction, leading to heated discussions about control and direction. Victoria may have viewed Jordan as a threat to her authority. Jordan's ambition and desire to expose hidden truths about the family's history intensified this rivalry. Their differing personalities—Jordan's assertiveness versus Victoria's controlling nature—fueled personal animosities, making their interactions strained and contentious.

Moreover, Victoria's fierce protectiveness over the family and the estate likely stemmed from her fear of losing everything she had worked for. This need to protect her legacy drove her to see Jordan as an obstacle rather than a family member. Despite the rivalry, there may have been moments when Victoria felt a sense of obligation or affection for Jordan, leading to internal conflict. She might have felt responsible for guiding Jordan but struggled with the fear of being usurped. The tension reached its peak during the event, where Victoria and Jordan likely had a heated argument. This confrontation may have stemmed from Jordan's intention to unveil family secrets, pushing Victoria to a breaking point. Overall, Victoria's relationship with Jordan was marked by a mix of rivalry, protection, and emotional conflict. While Victoria may have once cared for Jordan, her protective instincts and fear of losing control ultimately led her to view Jordan as a threat, culminating in the tragic events that unfolded.

Option 3: Accuse Liam

Liam Torres is not the murderer, and several key factors contribute to this conclusion.

Unlike Victoria, who had a clear interest in controlling the estate and protecting her legacy, Liam's motivations appear more self-serving. While he had a business relationship with Jordan, it was not inherently antagonistic. There's no evidence that Jordan posed a significant threat to Liam's interests, making a murder motive less likely. Liam was in the study preparing for his speech when Jordan collapsed. His demeanor during the investigation suggests a level of detachment and perhaps even relief rather than guilt or concern. While he may have disliked Jordan, his reaction indicates that he was not involved in their death. Liam's responses during the interviews lacked the emotional weight associated with guilt. His comments about Jordan's potential overreaction indicate he did not perceive them as a serious threat to his business interests. If he were the murderer, one would expect more anxiety or defensiveness in his demeanor.

Liam and Jordan had a professional dynamic characterized by occasional tension. They likely interacted frequently due to their roles within the family estate's management, which involved joint decisions and negotiations. However, this relationship was primarily transactional rather than personal. There was an underlying mutual dislike between Liam and Jordan, but it stemmed more from differing approaches to business than from personal animosity. Jordan's ambition and assertiveness contrasted sharply with Liam's more laid-back attitude, leading to friction but not outright hostility. Liam may have felt overshadowed by Jordan's ambitions, especially if Jordan sought to introduce changes that could impact the business. However, this conflict did not reach the level of personal vendetta, making murder unlikely. Liam seemed more focused on self-preservation than on eliminating perceived threats. His behavior during the event and throughout the investigation reflected a desire to maintain his position rather than take extreme measures against Jordan. In summary, while Liam had a complicated relationship with Jordan marked by professional rivalry and personal dislike, the absence of a compelling motive, combined with his alibi and demeanor during the investigation, firmly placed him outside the circle of suspicion. He was more concerned about the implications of Jordan's actions on his business than about resorting to violence.

Option 4: Accuse Riley

Riley Harrison is not the murderer, and several factors clarify why this is the case.

Riley was with other guests in a separate area when Jordan collapsed. Multiple witnesses can vouch for Riley's presence during the critical moment, providing a solid alibi that makes it implausible for them to have committed the murder. Riley's relationship with Jordan was predominantly positive, rooted in friendship. There's no evidence of animosity or conflict between them, making a motive for murder unlikely. Riley's reaction to Jordan's death was one of shock and sadness, not fear or guilt. They expressed genuine concern for Jordan and the situation, which contrasts with the behavior typically exhibited by someone who has committed a crime. Unlike other characters, Riley does not have any clear motives that would drive them to harm Jordan. Their goals and ambitions do not conflict with Jordan's, eliminating the incentive for murder.

Riley and Jordan shared a close friendship, characterized by mutual support and understanding. They often confided in each other about their concerns regarding the family and the estate. This bond suggests a level of trust that makes betrayal through murder highly unlikely. Both Riley and Jordan had a vested interest in the well-being of the family estate, which fostered a collaborative spirit rather than competition. They likely collaborated on decisions regarding the estate, reinforcing their alliance. When tensions arose—such as disagreements regarding family matters or estate management—Riley tended to approach Jordan with a desire for dialogue and resolution, rather than aggression. This approach highlights their mutual respect and lack of hostile intent. Riley often acted as a protector for Jordan, particularly during challenging times. This dynamic suggests that Riley would be more inclined to defend Jordan against potential threats rather than harm them. In summary, Riley's alibi, positive relationship with Jordan, and emotional response to their death firmly place them outside the circle of suspicion. Their friendship and shared interests indicate that Riley would be more likely to stand by Jordan than betray them.

Option 5: Accuse Alex

Detective Alex Reynolds is not the murderer, and several key factors support this conclusion.

As a seasoned investigator, Alex has a strong commitment to upholding the law and seeking justice. Their professionalism suggests that they would never compromise their integrity by committing murder, especially in a situation where they would later be tasked with investigating the crime. Alex is actively leading the investigation, analyzing evidence, and questioning suspects. Their role is to uncover the truth, not to obscure it. This duality makes it highly unlikely that Alex would have committed the crime, as doing so would undermine their own authority and credibility. Throughout the investigation, Alex maintains a level of emotional detachment, focusing on the facts rather than personal feelings. This behavior indicates a professional mindset that is inconsistent with committing murder, which typically involves heightened emotions and impulsive actions. There is no clear motive for Alex to harm Jordan. Their primary objective is to solve the case and bring justice, not to create further chaos or conflict. As an investigator, Alex has no personal stake in the family dynamics that would lead to murder.

Alex's relationship with Jordan was primarily professional. They may have interacted during previous investigations or social events, but there was no significant personal connection or animosity between them. Jordan likely respected Alex's role as a detective, viewing them as someone who could provide assistance rather than as an adversary. This mutual respect reduces the likelihood of any underlying conflict. Alex viewed Jordan as a victim rather than a suspect. Their focus is on gathering evidence to solve the case, not on harboring ill will. This objective perspective further distances Alex from any potential motive to commit murder. During interviews, Alex exhibits no signs of hostility or animosity toward Jordan. Instead, their focus is on understanding the circumstances surrounding the death, indicating a professional demeanor rather than personal involvement. In summary, Alex's strong professional integrity, lack of motive, and primarily professional relationship with Jordan firmly establish them as an unlikely suspect. Their role as the investigator places them on the side of justice, making it implausible for them to be involved in Jordan's murder.

Option 6: Accuse a Hidden Guest

The hidden guest is not the murderer, and several reasons clarify this conclusion. The hidden guest's presence is shrouded in mystery, but their motives and intentions remain largely unknown. Without a clear motive or connection to Jordan, it's difficult to attribute the murder to them. Since the hidden guest is not part of the established social circle, their relationship with Jordan is non-existent. This lack of personal or professional ties eliminates any plausible motive for murder, making it unlikely that they would target Jordan specifically. The hidden guest may have been more interested in observing the event and the dynamics of the people involved rather than actively participating in the conflict. Their motivations could center around gathering information rather than causing harm. If the hidden guest were indeed present, they could inadvertently be a witness to the events surrounding Jordan's death. Committing murder in such a visible manner would be reckless for someone trying to stay under the radar. The hidden guest's stealthy presence may have limited their ability to interact with others and engage in actions that would lead to murder. If they were primarily focused on remaining unnoticed, committing a high-profile crime would contradict their intent.

Since the hidden guest was not part of the family or the close-knit group of friends, they had no direct interactions with Jordan. This absence of interaction eliminates any possibility of personal grievances or motives for murder. The hidden guest may have been curious about the family dynamics and the ongoing tensions within the group. Their interest likely stems from an external perspective rather than personal vendetta, making murder unlikely. As a hidden guest, they would be more inclined to observe the unfolding drama rather than get involved in it. This passive role further distances them from the motivations typically associated with committing murder. In summary, the hidden guest's unclear identity, lack of relationship with Jordan, and passive observational role make them an unlikely suspect in the murder. Their motivations seem more aligned with curiosity than with malice, firmly placing them outside the circle of suspicion.

Whodunit "Live" Your Thoughts

This is where you can write your thoughts about who you think killed Jordan. You can do this before making your decision or after. There are plenty of moments throughout to make your choice.

Season 2, Episode 2

The story opens with a lavish summer gala hosted at the prestigious seaside estate of Magnolia Harper, a high-society influencer and philanthropist known for her extravagant parties. Guests, dressed to impress, mingle along the estate's beautiful ocean view as music drifts through the salty air. However, the perfect evening takes a dark turn when a body is discovered floating in the pool.

Main Characters Present:

Detective Tobias Ward: A sharp-minded investigator with a dry sense of humor, Tobias doesn't let the beauty of the estate distract him. He's here for one reason: to get to the bottom of this murder. His relentless approach can unsettle even the calmest suspect.

"I don't care how fancy the party is—somebody's leaving in handcuffs."*

Magnolia Harper: The glamorous hostess, Magnolia, always puts on a grand show. But beneath her polished socialite persona, there are whispers about her ties to dubious business deals. Her shock at the murder feels real, but is it just another performance? "This was supposed to be a celebration, not a crime scene!"*

Rafe "Razor" Delgado: A mysterious guest, Rafe is a former boxer turned personal trainer, known for his intense persona. He was invited as Magnolia's special guest, though no one seems to know why he's really here. His short temper and rugged demeanor make him stand out. "I was nowhere near the pool. Why would I kill someone at a party like this?"*

Esme Calderon

The heiress to a massive fashion empire, Esme is beautiful, calculating, and always dressed to perfection. Her family's wealth has allowed her to keep secrets well-hidden. She claims to have no connection to the victim, but her evasive answers raise suspicion. "I barely knew them. This is all just... too much."*

Theo Munroe

A tech genius who made millions developing a popular app, Theo is socially awkward but incredibly smart. He's always observing, analyzing, and rarely speaks unless he has to. His presence at such a social event is unusual, but is there more to his story? "I've seen a lot of things, but I never thought I'd see someone murdered at a party."*

Talia Quinn: Magnolia's longtime friend and assistant, Talia is fiercely loyal but often overlooked. She was in charge of organizing the entire event, running around in the background to ensure everything went smoothly. But she knew the victim better than she lets on. "I was just trying to make sure everything was perfect. I didn't even know something was wrong until I saw the body."

Act 1: The Discovery

As guests sip their cocktails and chat about business and pleasure, a scream pierces the air. Someone has spotted a body drifting lifelessly in the pool, face down. Panic erupts. Magnolia Harper gasps and rushes to the edge of the water, but it's too late—the victim is already gone.

Act 2: The Investigation Begins

Detective Tobias Ward arrives on the scene, wasting no time in securing the area. The glamorous setting doesn't distract him—his focus is solely on unraveling the mystery. The victim, Lennox Adler, wasn't just any partygoer; he had connections to several of the attendees.

Tobias starts with questioning the key suspects:

Magnolia Harper:

Tobias: *"You invited him here tonight. What was your connection to Lennox?"*

Magnolia: *"Lennox was a guest, like everyone else. I had no reason to want him dead. I'm as shocked as anyone."*

Tobias: *"Hosting the party gives you the perfect cover. Did you have a personal or professional reason to want him out of the picture?"*

Magnolia: *"Professional? Maybe. But nothing worth killing over. This is absurd!"*

Rafe Delgado:

Tobias: *"You and Lennox had a confrontation earlier in the evening. Witnesses say it got heated."*

Rafe: *"Yeah, we had words, but it wasn't about me. He was saying some things about Magnolia. I was just defending her honor."*

Tobias: *"You've got quite the reputation, Delgado. Ever considered that your temper might have taken it too far?"*

Rafe: *"I didn't lay a hand on him. Look somewhere else."*

Esme Calderon:

Tobias: *"You claim not to know Lennox well, but your paths have crossed. Care to elaborate?"*

Esme: *"We ran in the same circles. But I had no business with him. I'm just here to enjoy the party."*

Tobias: *"Is that so? Or were you trying to avoid someone who knew too much about your family's skeletons?"*

Esme: *"Watch your tone, Detective. I don't appreciate accusations without evidence."*

Theo Munroe:

Tobias: *"You're the quiet type, Theo. Always watching. What did you see tonight?"*

Theo: *"I'm a tech guy, not a socialite. But I did notice Lennox arguing with someone before things went south. I just couldn't hear who it was."*

Tobias: *"You're sharp, Theo. Don't hold back now. Any idea what the argument was about?"*

Theo: *"Something about money. But I don't have details."*

Talia Quinn:

Tobias: *"You seem pretty shaken, Talia. Nervous about something?"*

Talia: *"No! I mean, yes. It's just... I didn't expect this to happen at the party I helped plan."* Tobias: *"You knew Lennox better than the others, didn't you? What aren't you telling me?"* Talia: *"Lennox and I... we had a history. But I swear I didn't kill him. I wouldn't."*

Option 1: Accuse Magnolia Harper

Option 2: Accuse Rafe "Razor" Delgado

Option 3: Accuse Esme Calderon

Option 4: Accuse Theo Munroe

Option 5: Accuse Talia Quinn

Whodunit "Live" Your Thoughts

This is where you can write your thoughts about who you think killed Lennox. You can do this before making your decision or after. There are plenty of moments throughout to make your choice.

Option 1: Accuse Magnolia Harper

If you chose Magnolia Harper, you'd be correct! Magnolia Harper had the most to lose with Lennox Adler's untimely death. As the host of the grand gala, she had a close relationship with Lennox, who had recently uncovered her illegal financial activities. Lennox had planned to expose her crimes—embezzlement and fraudulent dealings with her charitable foundation—at the event, choosing the gala's spotlight to unveil her deception. Magnolia knew that if Lennox followed through, her carefully curated reputation, her business empire, and her social standing would be in ruins. The confrontation between them occurred near the pool, where Lennox threatened to publicly announce her crimes. In a moment of panic and desperation, Magnolia pushed him. He hit his head on the pool's edge and drowned in the water. Though she didn't plan on killing him, her actions were driven by fear and a need to protect her legacy. Magnolia's cold demeanor throughout the investigation and the slip-ups during her interview—her visible unease when Lennox's name was mentioned and her inconsistent statements—made her guilt clear to Detective Tobias Ward.

Option 2: Accuse Rafe "Razor" Delgado

Rafe "Razor" Delgado is not the murderer, and several key factors support this conclusion. Rafe, a known hothead with a sharp tongue, seemed like a strong suspect due to his very public argument with Lennox. But as much as Rafe despised Lennox for stirring trouble, he was not the murderer. Rafe was angry because Lennox was bad-mouthing Magnolia, and Rafe, who had his own business dealings with her, didn't appreciate Lennox's insinuations. However, despite his fiery personality, Rafe didn't have a motive strong enough to kill Lennox. His loyalty to Magnolia was about protecting their mutual interests, not eliminating people who posed a threat to her. His argument with Lennox was loud and heated, but ultimately, it was just a verbal clash that led nowhere.

Option 3: Accuse Esme Calderon

Esme Calderon is not the murderer, and several key factors support this conclusion. Esme Calderon, the wealthy heiress, also had a strained relationship with Lennox. He had represented her family in several legal matters and knew more about their secrets than Esme was comfortable with. But despite the tension, Esme was far too calculated to kill Lennox at such a public event. She believed in using her influence and money to deal with problems behind closed doors, not in broad daylight. Her alibi held up under scrutiny, and while her business interests may have been threatened, they weren't directly linked to Lennox's murder. Esme had no reason to confront Lennox that night, and her cool demeanor suggested she had nothing to hide.

Option 4: Accuse Theo Munroe

Theo Munroe is not the murderer, and several key factors support this conclusion. Theo, the introverted tech genius, might have seemed like the perfect candidate to commit a murder in the shadows. Quiet, analytical, and often overlooked, Theo knew how to stay under the radar. But despite his social awkwardness, he had no real connection to Lennox. Theo had been invited to the party for business reasons, not personal ones, and he was more interested in his gadgets than the human drama surrounding him. His tech background made him an asset in unraveling clues, but he didn't have the motive or opportunity to kill Lennox. Besides, Theo was found mingling with guests far from the pool at the time of the murder.

Option 5: Accuse Talia Quinn

Talia Quinn is not the murderer, and several key factors support this conclusion. Talia had a complicated history with Lennox, and their past romantic entanglement made her a suspect when Lennox turned up dead. There was no love lost between them—Lennox had broken Talia's heart, and their relationship ended on bad terms. But as much as Talia resented him, she had moved on from their tumultuous relationship. She didn't stand to gain anything from Lennox's death. In fact, Talia's emotional reaction during the investigation proved she was devastated by his passing, not relieved. Her breakdown and grief were genuine, and it was clear that while she had loved him once, she had no hand in his murder.

Whodunit "Live" Your Thoughts

This is where you can write your thoughts about who you think killed Lennox. You can do this before making your decision or after. There are plenty of moments throughout to make your choice.

Season 2, Episode 3: "The Art of Deception"

The episode takes place at The Hargrave Museum of Contemporary Art, where an exclusive exhibition is being held. The elite of the art world are gathered for the unveiling of an extraordinary collection by a mysterious, reclusive artist known only as **Seraphine**. The museum is filled with paintings, sculptures, and avant-garde installations, and guests move through the space sipping cocktails and making small talk.

Julian Rhodes is a wealthy art dealer who was known for his ruthless business tactics. He brokered multi-million-dollar deals and was often accused of stealing credit for major art acquisitions. While influential, Julian made enemies in the process. On the night of the exhibition, Julian was found dead in the museum's private viewing room, just before the collection was revealed to the public. He was strangled with a velvet rope used to section off the exhibit.

The Main Characters:

Aurelia St. James: The elegant and ambitious curator of The Hargrave Museum. She had a complicated history with Julian. Rumor has it that he sabotaged one of her deals in the past, costing her a prized exhibition.

Cassian "Cass" Locke: A famous yet controversial art critic who had a public feud with Julian. Cass often accused Julian of inflating the value of mediocre art to scam clients, and their rivalry was well-known in the art world.

Seraphine (real name unknown: The enigmatic artist whose works are being exhibited. She never shows her face at public events and communicates only through her agent. Some believe that Seraphine's identity has been hidden for a reason, and Julian was said to know her true identity.

Natalia "Nate" Durant: Seraphine's loyal agent. Nate is known for being protective of her client's identity and work. She has a no-nonsense attitude and always seemed to be at odds with Julian, who had attempted to buy out Seraphine's collection several times, much to Nate's frustration.

Alec Brandt: A former artist turned art dealer who had been blacklisted by Julian after a public falling out. Alec's career suffered greatly because of Julian's influence in the art world, and he harbored a deep grudge against him.

Act 1: The Discovery of the Body

As the guests move through the exhibit, the atmosphere is one of excitement and mystery. Suddenly, there's a loud gasp from the private viewing room. A museum staff member stumbles out, calling for help. Julian's lifeless body is found on the floor, the velvet rope wrapped tightly around his neck. Detective Tobias Ward arrives on the scene and begins questioning the guests. Julian's death, occurring in such an exclusive and high-profile setting, sends shockwaves through the crowd. The art world's most influential figures are now suspects, and as the investigation begins, it becomes clear that many had reasons to want Julian dead.

Act 2: The Investigation Begins

Detective Tobias Ward, already a seasoned investigator from the previous murders, is no stranger to high-society crimes. He immediately starts questioning the key suspects, uncovering their secrets and motives.

Aurelia St. James: Aurelia's career had been deeply affected by Julian's underhanded tactics. She had once been poised to host an exhibit that would have cemented her position in the art world, but Julian had swooped in and ruined her chances. When asked about her relationship with Julian, Aurelia remains poised but slips when discussing the rivalry. Did her desire for revenge finally push her to murder?

Cassian Locke: Cass had always been vocal about his disdain for Julian, both publicly and privately. Their feud had escalated over the years, with Cass frequently discrediting Julian's work in his reviews. Cass's alibi is shaky, and his knowledge of the museum layout makes him a prime suspect. Did the rivalry go too far?

Seraphine (through Nate): Seraphine, though absent physically, looms large over the night. Julian was one of the few people rumored to know her true identity. It's possible he planned to expose her at the event, which would have shattered her carefully guarded mystique. Nate, acting on Seraphine's behalf, had clashed with Julian many times before. Did Seraphine, or Nate, feel threatened enough to kill?

Natalia "Nate" Durant: Nate's fierce loyalty to Seraphine is well-known, and she had never been fond of Julian's aggressive attempts to acquire Seraphine's work. She had warned him multiple times to back off. Could Nate have killed Julian to protect Seraphine's secrets and her career?

Alec Brandt: Alec had lost everything after Julian ruined his career. His bitterness toward Julian was no secret, and he had been spotted near the private viewing room before the murder. Alec had the motive and the opportunity, but did he finally snap and seek vengeance?

As Detective Ward digs deeper, it becomes clear that everyone has something to hide. Aurelia's rivalry with Julian was more personal than she let on, and Cass had a private argument with Julian earlier in the night. Alec had the most obvious motive, but his alibi checks out. Nate's defense of Seraphine raises more questions about what Julian knew. The true culprit remains hidden as conflicting stories and secrets unravel. Who will be revealed as the killer in the art world's darkest night?

Option 1: Accuse Aurelia St. James
Option 2: Accuse Cassian "Cass" Locke
Option 3: Accuse Seraphine
Option 4: Accuse Natalia "Nate" Durant
Option 5: Accuse Alec Brandt

Whodunit "Live" Your Thoughts

This is where you can write your thoughts about who you think killed Julian. You can do this before making your decision or after. There are plenty of moments throughout to make your choice.

Option 1: Accuse Aurelia St. James

Aurelia St. James is not the murderer, and several key factors support this conclusion. Aurelia had plenty of reasons to hate Julian for ruining her career, but despite her cold, calculated exterior, she wasn't the one to kill him. Aurelia knew the art world too well, and she realized that killing Julian would do more harm than good for her reputation. She had worked too hard to get where she was and wouldn't risk everything for revenge. Her coldness toward Julian was just professional rivalry, nothing more. When pressed for details, her alibi held up, and she was too focused on her next big exhibition to be bothered with murder.

Option 2: Accuse Cassian "Cass" Locke

Cassian is not the murderer, and several key factors support this conclusion. Cassian's feud with Julian was fiery, but it was all about maintaining his credibility as an art critic. He loved his position of power in the art world and took pride in tearing down what he saw as "false" success, like Julian's inflated deals. Cass was an opportunist, and while he enjoyed publicly shaming Julian, murder wasn't part of his plan. In fact, Cass was busy giving a drunken critique of a painting during the time of the murder, loudly pontificating in front of witnesses who could vouch for his location.

Option 3: Accuse Seraphine

Seraphine is not the murderer, and several key factors support this conclusion. Seraphine, the elusive artist, had reasons to keep her identity hidden, and Julian's knowledge of her real name was troubling. However, Seraphine herself wasn't involved in the murder. She was too secretive and stayed far away from public events, operating from behind the scenes. Nate, acting on Seraphine's behalf, was protective but not violent. While Nate had exchanged words with Julian earlier in the night about backing off Seraphine, it didn't escalate to anything beyond harsh warnings. Nate was seen with other guests at the time of the murder, ensuring Seraphine's interests were protected but not through murder.

Option 4: Accuse Natalia "Nate" Durant

Natalia is not the murderer, and several key factors support this conclusion. Nate had the sharpest tongue and would do anything to protect her client's work and reputation. She had clashed with Julian many times in the past, and Julian's attempts to purchase Seraphine's collection infuriated her. But Nate was practical—she knew there were other ways to deal with Julian that didn't involve violence. Nate had too much riding on her professional reputation, and she was far too calculated to kill in such a public setting. When the time of death was established, Nate's alibi was rock-solid, as she was in the middle of negotiating deals with collectors elsewhere in the museum.

Option 5: Accuse Alec Brandt

If you chose Alec, you'd be correct! Alec had been simmering with rage ever since Julian Rhodes destroyed his career. As a once-promising artist, Alec had been on the verge of a breakthrough until Julian blacklisted him, leaving him unable to sell his work or gain any kind of recognition. With no options left, Alec was forced to give up his art and became a dealer, something he resented. When Alec found out that Julian would be at the gala, he saw it as his opportunity for revenge. The idea of confronting Julian had always been in the back of his mind, but that night, seeing Julian in his element, flaunting his power over the art world, drove Alec over the edge. Alec followed Julian into the private viewing room, where they had a heated argument. In a moment of rage and desperation, Alec grabbed the velvet rope and strangled Julian. Alec didn't plan the murder, but it became his way of reclaiming his dignity. His actions were impulsive, born from years of frustration and bitterness. Alec initially thought he'd get away with it, but his shaken demeanor during questioning, coupled with a slip in his alibi, made him a prime suspect for Detective Ward.

Whodunit "Live" Your Thoughts

This is where you can write your thoughts about who you think killed Julian. You can do this before making your decision or after. There are plenty of moments throughout to make your choice.

Season 2, Episode 4

The episode takes place at The Delacourt Opera House, an opulent, historic venue hosting the premiere of a much-anticipated performance by world-renowned soprano Livia Monterosso. The crème de la crème of high society is in attendance, dressed in their finest attire. The grandeur of the opera house, with its gold-leaf embellishments and velvet seating, contrasts sharply with the tragedy about to unfold. Livia Monterosso, the legendary soprano, is found dead backstage just moments before she is due to take the stage. She has been poisoned—her tea, a routine part of her pre-performance ritual, was laced with a deadly substance. Livia's death not only shocks the opera world but also the city's elite, as she was at the height of her fame, with no clear enemies in sight. But as Detective Tobias Ward soon discovers, not everything is as it seems, and Livia had secrets of her own.

The Main Characters:

Beatrix "Bea" Stone: The fiercely ambitious understudy to Livia. Bea had always resented living in Livia's shadow, never quite able to step into the limelight. Did she see this as her one chance to take over the starring role?

Raoul Cavendish: The opera's temperamental conductor. Known for his perfectionism, Raoul had frequent clashes with Livia over her creative choices. While he admired her talent, their power struggles often spilled into rehearsals. Was Raoul's frustration with Livia's diva behavior enough to lead to murder?

Lucien Armand: A wealthy patron of the arts and Livia's secret lover. Lucien had been supporting Livia's career financially for years, though their relationship was hidden from the public eye. Recently, their romance had been strained, with rumors that Livia was planning to end things. Did Lucien's love for Livia turn into a deadly obsession?

Valentina Costas: Livia's longtime assistant and confidante. Valentina knew everything about Livia's life, from her professional struggles to her personal secrets. Valentina had devoted years of her life to Livia, but their relationship had become tense lately. Could Valentina have decided that Livia was no longer worth protecting?

Nico Marin: A rising star tenor who had recently joined the opera company. Nico admired Livia, but there were whispers of an affair between them, which complicated his relationship with Beatrix. Could jealousy have driven Nico to eliminate Livia?

Act 1: The Discovery of the Body

The performance is about to begin when a stagehand finds Livia Monterosso collapsed in her dressing room, a half-empty cup of tea beside her. Panic spreads as it becomes clear that Livia is dead, the victim of poisoning. Detective Tobias Ward is called in to investigate, once again stepping into the world of high-society drama and dangerous secrets. The investigation begins with Detective Ward interviewing the cast and crew of the opera, all of whom seem shocked by Livia's death. However, it quickly becomes apparent that beneath the glamorous surface, tensions had been building backstage, and nearly everyone had a reason to want Livia out of the picture.

Act 2: The Investigation

As the detective unravels the web of relationships surrounding Livia, suspicions fall on several key players.

Bea had spent years waiting for her moment in the spotlight, always second to Livia. While publicly she praised Livia's talent, behind closed doors, there were whispers of envy and resentment. With Livia dead, Bea would now take center stage. During questioning, Bea appears calm, too calm, perhaps, for someone who just lost her mentor. But did her jealousy go far enough to kill?

Raoul Cavendish:

Raoul's frequent clashes with Livia were no secret. He found her impossible to work with, and their arguments had escalated recently as they disagreed on the direction of the performance. Raoul had a reputation for being volatile, and Livia had threatened to leave the production altogether. Could his ego and desire to maintain control over his masterpiece have led him to murder?

Lucien Armand:

Lucien had been financing Livia's career, and their romantic relationship was an open secret in the upper echelons of society. However, their relationship had recently cooled, with Livia pulling away. Lucien had been heard arguing with Livia backstage the night before her death. Was Lucien's pride and love for Livia turned into a deadly obsession, or was he simply heartbroken?

Valentina Costas:

Valentina was the one person who knew all of Livia's deepest secrets. She had stood by Livia's side for years, managing her life and career. However, in recent weeks, their relationship had soured, and Livia had hinted at firing Valentina after the performance. Valentina's devotion could have turned into bitterness and betrayal—was this her revenge for years of thankless work?

Accusing Nico Marin:

Nico, the charming young tenor, had always idolized Livia. But rumors of an affair between them threatened his standing with the rest of the company, especially his complicated relationship with Bea. Could Nico have decided that Livia was more of a threat than an ally, and poisoned her to protect his future?

Detective Ward discovers that Livia's tea had been poisoned with a rare and fast-acting substance, something that only a few people in the opera house could have accessed. The investigation narrows down the suspects based on opportunity and motive, but as with every case, red herrings abound. Some characters seem too obvious—Beatrix's jealousy is apparent, and Raoul's arguments with Livia were public knowledge. But as Ward digs deeper, it becomes clear that the real murderer had carefully planned the crime to make it look like someone else's fault.

Option 1: Accuse Beatrix "Bea" Stone
Option 2: Accuse Raoul Cavendish
Option 3: Accuse Lucien Armand
Option 4: Accuse Valentina Costas
Option 5: Accuse Nico Marin

Whodunit "Live" Your Thoughts

This is where you can write your thoughts about who you think killed Livia. You can do this before making your decision or after. There are plenty of moments throughout to make your choice.

Option 1: Accuse Beatrix "Bea" Stone

While Bea had long envied Livia for the spotlight, she wasn't a killer. Her ambition was strong, but she was more focused on proving herself through her talent, not through violent means. During the investigation, it became clear that Bea didn't have the opportunity to tamper with Livia's tea, as she was busy with last-minute rehearsals and preparing for her understudy role. Bea was frustrated, but she wasn't desperate enough to commit murder.

Option 2: Accuse Raoul Cavendish

Raoul, the volatile conductor, had his share of arguments with Livia. They had clashed over creative control, but Raoul was far too focused on his work to resort to violence. He was known for being strict, but not cruel. When interviewed, Raoul explained that his disagreements with Livia were purely professional, and witnesses confirmed he had been in rehearsals with the orchestra at the time Livia's tea was poisoned. His temper made him seem suspicious, but Raoul had nothing to gain from Livia's death.

Option 3: Accuse Lucien Armand

Lucien, the wealthy patron and secret lover, was heartbroken by Livia's death. Though their relationship had been strained recently, Lucien still cared deeply for her and had even tried to reconcile. He was seen arguing with her earlier, but the argument was about their future together, not a motive for murder. Lucien had no access to the backstage area where Livia's tea was kept, and he was found mingling with other guests when the poisoning occurred. His alibi and visible grief cleared him from suspicion

Option 4: Accuse Valentina Costas

Valentina had been Livia Monterosso's loyal assistant for years, managing everything from her schedule to her personal life. However, their relationship had grown strained over time. Livia had become more demanding and ungrateful, pushing Valentina to the edge. In recent weeks, Livia had even threatened to fire Valentina, cutting her off from the glamorous life she had grown accustomed to. Valentina had sacrificed her personal ambitions for Livia's success, and this was how she was repaid. Feeling betrayed, underappreciated, and knowing her time with Livia was coming to an end, Valentina saw the poison as her only way out. She had access to Livia's dressing room and prepared her tea every night. Valentina made the decision to poison Livia's tea on the night of the performance, hoping to be rid of her former boss once and for all. The murder was premeditated, but Valentina masked it well, pretending to be devastated when Livia was found dead.

Option 5: Accuse Nico Marin

Nico admired Livia and had no reason to harm her. Despite rumors of an affair, Nico's relationship with Livia was purely professional. His budding romance with Bea might have caused tension, but Nico had been entirely focused on his performance that night. He had been seen with several cast members in the hours leading up to the murder, rehearsing his role. Nico was ambitious, but his goal was to rise through talent, not eliminate competition through murder.

Whodunit "Live" Your Thoughts

This is where you can write your thoughts about who you think killed Livia. You can do this before making your decision or after. There are plenty of moments throughout to make your choice.

Season 2, Episode 5

The Glenwood Estate, a luxurious, sprawling manor, is hosting an exclusive silent auction for the city's wealthiest elites. Priceless art, rare artifacts, and historical heirlooms are all up for grabs, with fierce competition brewing among the bidders. The air is thick with tension, as everyone seems to have their eyes on one particular item—a mysterious, centuries-old necklace rumored to carry a dark curse.

Frederick Hawthorne, a renowned art collector and philanthropist, is found dead in the library of the Glenwood Estate, the very room where the most coveted auction item, the cursed necklace, had been on display just hours earlier. Frederick had been one of the top bidders for the necklace, and rumors swirled that he intended to use it for some secretive personal project. But now, he lies dead, the necklace missing, and the auction is halted as Detective Tobias Ward arrives to piece together what happened. Frederick's death is no accident—he was found with a glass of wine in hand, but a quick analysis reveals that the wine had been poisoned. The question is: who among the auction attendees wanted Frederick dead, and what does the missing necklace have to do with it?

Cecilia "Cece" Monroe: A high-powered art dealer with a penchant for cutthroat deals. Cece had been vying for the necklace herself and wasn't pleased that Frederick had outbid her. She's known for using any means necessary to secure the items she desires—did her competitive nature drive her to murder?

Julian Cross: A historian specializing in ancient artifacts, Julian had been consulted about the necklace's history and had warned the auction house about its rumored curse. Some believed he was overly dramatic, but Julian seemed to have a personal stake in ensuring the necklace stayed out of the wrong hands. Could his obsession with protecting history have led him to kill?

Rosalind "Roz" Clayton: A wealthy socialite and Frederick's longtime rival. Roz had always resented Frederick for his success in the art world, particularly because he had outmaneuvered her on numerous acquisitions. The auction was supposed to be her chance to finally beat him. Was Roz's rivalry strong enough to motivate her to murder?

Daniel Hawthorne: Frederick's nephew and the sole heir to his vast fortune. Daniel and Frederick had a strained relationship, with Frederick often belittling Daniel's lack of ambition. With Frederick out of the way, Daniel stands to inherit everything. Was Daniel's resentment and desire for wealth the reason for Frederick's death?

Helena Sterling: A reclusive artist whose painting was also up for auction. Helena's work had been overshadowed by the interest in the cursed necklace, which enraged her. She had been a close friend of Frederick's, but rumors suggested that their relationship had recently soured. Could Helena's fragile ego and recent falling-out with Frederick have led her to poison him?

Act 1: The Discovery of the Body

Frederick's body is found shortly after the guests are seated for dinner. His death causes immediate chaos, especially as it's discovered that the necklace—the most sought-after item at the auction—has vanished. Detective Tobias Ward is called in to investigate, with suspicion falling on the guests who had been bidding against Frederick for the necklace. Everyone had seen him sipping wine throughout the night, but no one had noticed when it turned deadly.

Act 2: The Investigation

Interview with Cecilia "Cece" Monroe

Detective Ward: "Miss Monroe, you had quite a visible reaction when you lost the auction to Frederick Hawthorne. Can you walk me through what happened after that?"

Cecilia Monroe: *stiff, composed* "Frustration, of course. Losing an important piece to someone like Frederick? It stung. But I'm not a murderer, Detective. It's business, not personal."

Detective Ward: "You said earlier you had to step out during the auction to take a call. Can you confirm where you were when Mr. Hawthorne was poisoned?"

Cecilia Monroe: "I was outside, speaking with a client. You can check my call logs."

Detective Ward: "Did you have any direct confrontations with Mr. Hawthorne after the auction?"

Cecilia Monroe: *sighs* "No. The moment I saw that necklace slip away, I knew it wasn't my night. There was nothing more to be said."

Interview with Julian Cross

Detective Ward: "Mr. Cross, your fascination with the cursed necklace has been well noted. Did you ever speak to Mr. Hawthorne directly about it?"

Julian Cross: *intense, almost jittery* "Of course I did! I warned him. I told him it wasn't just a trinket to be hoarded away. He didn't care. He laughed at me, Detective."

Detective Ward: "You left the auction hall for some time. Why?"

Julian Cross: "I needed air. Frederick's arrogance—it was suffocating. He had no respect for history, for what that artifact represented."

Detective Ward: "So, did you confront him about his purchase?"

Julian Cross: *nervous laughter* "Confront? No, no. I wouldn't... I didn't kill him, if that's what you're asking. But I won't lie—part of me is relieved he didn't live long enough to desecrate that artifact."

Interview with Rosalind "Roz" Clayton

Detective Ward: "Ms. Clayton, it's known that you and Mr. Hawthorne were bitter rivals in the art world. How do you feel about losing to him again?"

Roz Clayton: *cool, self-assured* "I'm no stranger to losing bids, Detective. It's part of the game. Frederick and I had a professional rivalry, nothing more."

Detective Ward: "Yet, multiple guests reported seeing you storm out just before the incident."

Roz Clayton: *chuckles* "Oh, I was furious, yes. But only because I knew Frederick was going to gloat. I didn't leave the auction to poison him, though. I was gathering myself—getting some fresh air."

Detective Ward: "Was there any reason you'd want to harm him outside of this auction?"

Roz Clayton: "Frederick was obnoxious, but I wouldn't throw my career and reputation away over a petty win."

Interview with Daniel Hawthorne

Detective Ward: "Mr. Hawthorne, losing your uncle must be difficult. How would you describe your relationship with him?"

Daniel Hawthorne: *shifty, nervous* "Frederick and I... we had our issues. He was hard on me, always pushing me to be something I'm not. But he was family, Detective. You don't kill family."

Detective Ward: "You were seen stepping out onto the terrace around the time of his death. Can anyone verify that?"

Daniel Hawthorne: *pauses, uneasy* "I was alone. I needed a breather. Frederick was... he was getting on my nerves. But I didn't hurt him."

Detective Ward: "Your uncle's death benefits you financially. Did that thought cross your mind?"

Daniel Hawthorne: *defensive* "I didn't kill him! Yes, I'll inherit, but that doesn't mean I'd poison my own uncle!"

Interview with Helena Sterling:

Detective Ward: "Ms. Sterling, your work was one of the highlights of the auction. Did Frederick's winning the necklace overshadow your presentation?"

Helena Sterling: *frustrated* "Of course, it did. But it wasn't Frederick's fault, not really. I was upset, but that's on me."

Detective Ward: "Witnesses say you were seen leaving in a hurry before Frederick's death. Where did you go?"

Helena Sterling: *somber* "I needed a moment. I was backstage, getting ready for my presentation, and the whole necklace thing threw me off. I didn't want to see anyone."

Detective Ward: "You and Frederick were close at one point, but had recently fallen out. Can you tell me about that?"

Helena Sterling: *sighs* "We disagreed over some personal matters, but I didn't kill him, Detective. We'd argued, yes, but nothing serious enough to lead to murder."

OPTION 1: ACCUSE CECILIA "Cece" Monroe
    Option 2: Accuse Julian Cross
    Option 3: Accuse Rosalind "Roz" Clayton
    Option 4: Accuse Daniel Hawthorne
    Option 5: Accuse Helena Sterling

Whodunit "Live" Your Thoughts

This is where you can write your thoughts about who you think killed Fredrick. You can do this before making your decision or after. There are plenty of moments throughout to make your choice.

Option 1: Accuse Cecilia "Cece" Monroe

Cecilia is not the murderer, and several key factors support this conclusion. Cece states that during the time of Frederick's death, she was in a heated phone conversation with one of her clients, who was demanding updates on another deal. Her assistant confirms that she was on a call, though no one can corroborate her exact location during the time Frederick's wine was poisoned. Cece's ambition and history of ruthless tactics could indicate she was willing to go to great lengths to get what she wanted, but the poison seems too messy for someone who typically plays by the rules of business—even if those rules are brutal. Cece's alibi is plausible, but she had the opportunity to tamper with the wine while making herself scarce. While her motives seem strong, the murder feels too personal for a cold, calculated dealer like Cece. The killer may have had more emotional investment.

Option 2: Accuse Julian Cross

Julian is not the murderer, and several key factors support this conclusion. Julian admits he had left the auction briefly to make a phone call outside, but no one can confirm where he went or who he spoke with. Julian claims he didn't want anyone to have the necklace, especially someone like Frederick, who he believed had no respect for its historical significance. Could Julian's desperation to protect the artifact have driven him to murder? Julian's obsession with the necklace makes him an easy suspect, but he doesn't seem the type to poison someone. His fixation was more on preserving history than on harming people. However, his shaky alibi and his eccentric personality make him difficult to rule out entirely.

Option 3: Accuse Rosalind "Roz" Clayton

Rosalind is not the murderer, and several key factors support this conclusion. Roz claims she was speaking with several guests at the time of Frederick's death, but no one recalls seeing her during the crucial moments when the poison could have been administered. Roz's rivalry with Frederick could easily have pushed her over the edge, especially since this auction was her chance to finally outshine him. Roz had both the motive and the opportunity, but her demeanor suggests she's more frustrated than vengeful. Her rivalry with Frederick was certainly intense, but Roz seems too focused on maintaining her reputation to resort to murder. Still, her lack of a solid alibi keeps her in the detective's sights.

Option 4: Accuse Daniel Hawthorne

If you chose Daniel, you'd be correct! Daniel insists that he was outside on the terrace during the time of Frederick's death, taking a break from the auction. However, no one can confirm his whereabouts, and his alibi is weak at best. With Frederick out of the way, Daniel would finally have the freedom and wealth he always desired. But was his resentment strong enough to drive him to murder? Daniel's weak alibi and clear motive make him a prime suspect. He had everything to gain from his uncle's death, and their strained relationship had been a source of tension for years. The detective keeps a close eye on Daniel, knowing that his financial motive could be the key to solving the case. Daniel's resentment toward his uncle had been festering for years. Frederick's constant belittling had pushed Daniel to the edge, and with the vast fortune and estate on the line, Daniel saw his opportunity. He poisoned Frederick's wine during a moment when no one was watching, hoping to inherit the family's wealth and finally break free of his uncle's shadow. Daniel had no solid alibi, and the financial motive was clear. The strained relationship and the arguments leading up to the murder were enough for Daniel to snap. He saw the auction as his chance to change his life, and he took it—at the cost of his uncle's.

Option 5: Accuse Helena Sterling

Helena is not the murderer, and several key factors support this conclusion. Helena claims she had been backstage preparing for her own presentation and hadn't seen Frederick since earlier in the evening. However, witnesses recall seeing Helena leave the room in a fury just before the murder. Helena may have been angry that her work was being overshadowed by the necklace, but was that anger enough to kill her longtime friend? Helena's artistic temperament and recent arguments with Frederick make her seem like a plausible suspect, but her passion for her work doesn't align with the cold, calculated nature of poisoning. Still, her outburst before the murder and her shaky alibi raise red flags.

Whodunit "Live" Your Thoughts

This is where you can write your thoughts about who you think killed Fredrick. You can do this before making your decision or after. There are plenty of moments throughout to make your choice.

Season 2, Episode 6

The scene opens at a lavish charity gala, hosted by the ever-charismatic philanthropist Nathaniel "Nate" Kingsley, whose reputation for generosity and high-society connections precedes him. The grand ballroom is filled with the city's elite, all gathered to raise funds for a cause close to Nate's heart: cancer research. But amidst the glamorous evening, tragedy strikes when Nate is found dead in his private office, a glass of champagne still in hand. As the clock strikes midnight, the lights flicker dramatically before plunging the room into darkness. When the lights return, a hush falls over the crowd. Nate's body is discovered by his assistant, **Eva Brooks**, and chaos quickly spreads through the event.

Main Characters:

Nathaniel "Nate" Kingsley (Victim): The wealthy and well-connected philanthropist who seemingly had no enemies. Known for his kindness and involvement in charitable causes, Nate was beloved by many—or so it seemed.

Eva Brooks (Nate's Assistant): Eva has been Nate's personal assistant for five years and knows every detail of his life. She is fiercely loyal and has often been rumored to have a closer relationship with Nate than just business.

Cameron "Cam" Ross (Business Partner): Cam was Nate's close friend and business associate. They've run several ventures together, but recently, whispers have surfaced about tensions between them due to a failed project that cost them millions.

Lydia Fox (Ex-Girlfriend): Lydia is Nate's former lover, who left him under mysterious circumstances three years ago. She's a renowned art dealer, and some say she's never truly moved on from Nate.

Tristan Wells (Journalist): Known for his investigative journalism, Tristan has spent years covering the lives of the wealthy elite. He's written several exposés about the misdeeds of powerful men, and Nate was rumored to be his next subject.

Isabella "Izzy" Moreno (Chef): Izzy is the head chef for the gala, known for her impeccable culinary skills. She's been hired by Nate for multiple events, but there's more to their relationship than meets the eye.

Detective Grace Ward (Investigator): Seasoned and sharp, Grace arrives to the scene quickly, taking control of the chaotic situation. She begins to sift through the layers of glamour and secrets to get to the truth.

Act 1: The Discovery

The discovery of Nate's body sends shockwaves through the gala. Guests are asked to remain in the building, while Detective Grace Ward begins her preliminary investigation. The atmosphere is tense as whispers fill the room, each guest quietly assessing who among them could be capable of such an act. Detective Ward's attention quickly turns to the champagne glass clutched in Nate's hand. She orders the glass to be tested for poison.

Act 2: The Investigation Begins

Interview with Eva Brooks

Detective Ward: "Eva, you were the one to find Nate. What can you tell me about the last time you saw him?"

Eva Brooks: *tears in her eyes* "It was just before midnight. He had gone to his office to take a break from the crowd. I brought him the champagne myself. He didn't seem worried or upset—just tired."

Detective Ward: "Did Nate have any enemies that you're aware of?"

Eva Brooks: "No! Nate was loved by everyone. I mean, there were business tensions, but nothing that would lead to... this."

Interview with Cameron Ross

Detective Ward: "Mr. Ross, you've been Nate's business partner for years. How would you describe your relationship with him?"

Cameron Ross: *coolly* "Complicated. Nate was a visionary, but not all of his ideas were good ones. We had our disagreements, but nothing out of the ordinary."

Detective Ward: "There have been rumors of a failed project between you two. Can you tell me about that?"

Cameron Ross: *smirking* "Business is risky. We lost money, but we bounced back. No hard feelings, if that's what you're insinuating."

Interview with Lydia Fox

Detective Ward: "Lydia, you and Nate had a romantic history. Did things ever get... bitter between you two after the breakup?"

Lydia Fox: *calm, collected* "It ended years ago. I moved on, as did he. Our breakup was mutual, Detective."

Detective Ward: "And yet, you're still attending his gala."

Lydia Fox: *smiling coldly* "Nate and I remained friends. My art dealings often brought us into the same circles. There was no animosity."

Interview with Tristan Wells

Detective Ward: "Mr. Wells, I understand you're a journalist. Were you writing a story about Nate?"

Tristan Wells: *nervous laughter* "I was. But nothing too scandalous, I assure you. Nate was a philanthropist; there wasn't much dirt to dig up."

Detective Ward: "Rumor has it you were about to publish an exposé. Was there something Nate wanted hidden?"

Tristan Wells: "If I had something juicy, you would've seen it in print already. No, I was working on a puff piece, believe it or not."

Interview with Isabella "Izzy" Moreno

Detective Ward: "Izzy, you were in charge of the food for the evening. Can you confirm that the champagne Nate drank came from your kitchen?"

Izzy Moreno: *serious, calm* "Yes, but only Eva had direct access to it. I made sure everything was prepared perfectly, but I can't control what happens after it leaves my hands."

Detective Ward: "What was your relationship with Nate like?"

Izzy Moreno: *sighs* "We worked together a lot. I respected him, and he respected my work. That's all there was to it."

Option 1: Accuse Eva Brooks
Option 2: Accuse Cameron "Cam" Ross
Option 3: Accuse Lydia Fox
Option 4: Accuse Tristan Wells
Option 5: Accuse Isabella "Izzy" Moreno

Whodunit "Live" Your Thoughts

This is where you can write your thoughts about who you think killed Nathaniel. You can do this before making your decision or after. There are plenty of moments throughout to make your choice.

Option 1: Accuse Eva Brooks

If you chose Eva, you'd be correct! Eva had been Nathaniel Kingsley's personal assistant for five years, a position of deep trust and proximity. What appeared to be mere loyalty had evolved into something far more dangerous—a possessive obsession. Eva's relationship with Nate was built on the belief that she was the only one who truly understood and protected him. Over time, her loyalty became warped, and she developed a belief that the people closest to Nate—especially his business partners and even romantic interests—were only exploiting him. On the night of the gala, Eva had direct access to Nate's champagne. She was the one who brought it to him in his private office, away from prying eyes. After seeing him interact with several guests earlier in the evening, particularly Cameron and Lydia, Eva felt Nate was being pulled into harmful alliances. In her mind, Nate needed to be "saved" from the people around him who, she believed, were slowly ruining him. By poisoning Nate, she thought she could protect him from what she saw as a world full of betrayal. It was a twisted act of love. Eva had complete access to Nate and his personal office. She was the last person to see him alive, and she had control over his food and drink, particularly the poisoned champagne. Eva's possessive obsession with Nate and her perception that others were out to harm him drove her to murder. She believed no one could protect him better than her, and her growing paranoia made her feel that killing him was the only way to shield him from betrayal. During her interview, Eva was visibly emotional, not just from grief, but from guilt. She seemed overly defensive when asked about Nate's relationships with other people, indicating her jealousy and obsession. Her nervousness escalated when Detective Ward began to question her access to Nate and the champagne.

Option 2: Accuse Cameron "Cam" Ross

Cameron is not the murderer, and several key factors support this conclusion. Cameron Ross, Nate's long-time business partner, had a rocky professional relationship with Nate. The failed business venture that cost them millions was well-known, and many suspected that it created a wedge between them. However, despite the financial strain, Cameron had no reason to kill Nate. Their partnership, while tense at times, was mutually beneficial. Cameron was set to gain nothing from Nate's death. Cameron had been mingling with high-profile guests during the time Nate was poisoned. Several witnesses confirmed that he never left the main ballroom. Cameron and Nate's business ventures were ongoing, and despite a few failures, they had recently rebounded financially. Killing Nate would have destroyed their ventures and left Cameron without a way to rebuild his business. In his interview, Cameron was calm and rational, showing no signs of a man under pressure. He may have been frustrated with Nate's leadership, but it was clear that their relationship was professional, not personal.

Option 3: Accuse Lydia Fox

Lydia is not the murderer, and several key factors support this conclusion. Lydia Fox, Nate's ex-girlfriend, had a long history with him, which led some to suspect that old wounds may have driven her to murder. However, their breakup had been amicable, and Lydia had long since moved on. She was a prominent art dealer, and her continued attendance at Nate's events was purely for business purposes. There was no indication that Lydia had any unresolved bitterness toward Nate. Their relationship had ended on good terms, and both had moved on romantically and professionally. Lydia had nothing to gain from his death. Lydia was seen in full view of guests during the time Nate was poisoned, interacting with several high-profile individuals. She had no opportunity to administer the poison. During her interview, Lydia was poised and articulate. She was saddened by Nate's death but showed no emotional intensity that would suggest a personal vendetta or hidden anger. Her calm demeanor and clarity in addressing her past with Nate further ruled her out as a suspect.

Option 4: Accuse Tristan Wells

Tristan is not the murderer, and several key factors support this conclusion. Tristan Wells, a sharp investigative journalist, was rumored to be working on an exposé about Nate. This rumor led to speculation that Nate had secrets Tristan wanted to reveal, potentially leading to a fatal confrontation. However, this theory fell apart under closer scrutiny. Tristan admitted during his interview that he was working on a fluff piece about Nate, focusing on his philanthropic efforts rather than an exposé. He had no damaging information on Nate that would have led to a confrontation or motive for murder. Tristan had little contact with Nate throughout the evening. He spent most of his time speaking with other guests and, like the others, had no access to Nate's private office or his champagne. Tristan's nervous laughter during the interview stemmed from his awareness that he was being scrutinized as a suspect. However, his responses were consistent and aligned with his reputation as a journalist. He had nothing to hide and was more interested in covering the gala than in bringing harm to anyone.

Option 5: Accuse Isabella "Izzy" Moreno

Isabella is not the murderer, and several key factors support this conclusion. As the head chef for the event, Izzy Moreno had complete control over the kitchen and the food served during the gala. This made her a potential suspect, as she had access to everything Nate consumed. However, she was not the culprit. While Izzy controlled the kitchen, the champagne served to Nate was handled by Eva Brooks. Izzy's role was strictly in food preparation, and she had no interaction with Nate's personal drinks or private moments. Izzy and Nate's relationship was professional, and she had worked with him on numerous events. There was no animosity or personal connection that would lead her to kill him. Izzy was calm and collected during her interview. She was focused on her professional responsibilities and showed no signs of guilt or nervousness. Her responses were straightforward, and she demonstrated a clear line between her job and Nate's personal affairs.

Whodunit "Live" Your Thoughts

This is where you can write your thoughts about who you think killed Nathaniel. You can do this before making your decision or after. There are plenty of moments throughout to make your choice.

Season 2, Episode 7

The scene unfolds at the luxurious Bellecrest Hotel during its annual charity gala, a glittering event filled with high-profile guests, all basking in the glow of opulence. However, this evening of elegance takes a dark turn when tragedy strikes yet again.

Main Suspects:

Scarlett Blakewell: Donovan's estranged wife, known for her fiery personality and bitter public spats with Donovan. Rumor has it that their impending divorce was about to turn ugly, with Scarlett standing to lose a fortune.

Noah Hart: A business rival who had been locked in a bitter dispute with Donovan over a lucrative real estate deal. Noah had been gunning to take Donovan down for years.

Serena Monroe: Donovan's personal assistant, who had been by his side for the past eight years. A fiercely loyal woman, but there are whispers that Donovan was preparing to fire her over recent mistakes.

Jasper Gale: An up-and-coming real estate mogul and former protégé of Donovan, Jasper was once mentored by him but their relationship soured after Donovan publicly humiliated him during a deal gone wrong.

Elena Rhodes: Donovan's current girlfriend, a much younger socialite who many suspected was with him purely for his wealth. Elena was last seen having a heated argument with Donovan before his death.

The Investigation

Detective Ward returns to unravel the mystery once again. He starts with the interviews, slowly peeling back layers of lies, deceit, and hidden motives. As the investigation unfolds, it becomes clear that every suspect had a reason to want Donovan dead, but only one could be responsible for his murder.

The Interviews

Scarlett Blakewell:

Detective Ward: "Scarlett, you and Donovan were in the middle of a rather contentious divorce, correct?"

Scarlett: *bluntly* "Yes, and it was about to get worse. Donovan thought he could control me even after we separated. He had no idea who he was dealing with."

Detective Ward: "There are rumors that you stood to lose a considerable amount of money due to the prenuptial agreement. Were you aware of that?"

Scarlett: *with a smirk* "Oh, I was well aware. But trust me, if I wanted to get back at Donovan, I would've done it in court, not by killing him. I'm not that desperate."

Detective Ward: "Yet, you were overheard making some rather... intense comments about Donovan's future. Any reason for that?"

Scarlett: *leaning forward* "Words, Detective. We were in the middle of a divorce. Things were bound to get heated. But believe me, I wasn't going to throw away my chance at a big settlement by doing something stupid."

Noah Hart:

Detective Ward: "Noah, it's no secret that you and Donovan were rivals. Business deals, public disputes... it wasn't exactly a friendly competition, was it?"

Noah: *calmly* "Rivalry is part of the game, Detective. Donovan and I were competing for the same market. But just because we were competitors doesn't mean I wanted him dead."

Detective Ward: "You two had a very public argument over a deal just weeks ago. Some say you were furious when Donovan outbid you. How do you explain that?"

Noah: *shrugging*

"I was angry, sure. Losing a deal like that hurts. But murder? That's not how I handle my losses. I have other ways to bounce back."

Detective Ward: "And yet, you knew Donovan's favorite drink, didn't you? You could have easily slipped something into it during the gala."

Noah: *narrowing his eyes* "Yes, I knew his drink preference—just like everyone else in the industry. But I don't poison people. I beat them in the boardroom, not by breaking the law."

Serena Monroe:

Detective Ward: "Serena, you worked for Donovan for eight years. That's a long time to stay by someone's side. How would you describe your relationship?"

Serena: *wiping her eyes*

"Donovan was... demanding. But I respected him. He gave me opportunities I wouldn't have had otherwise."

Detective Ward: "Opportunities that were about to end, I hear. There are whispers that Donovan was planning to let you go. Did you know that?"

Serena: *her face tightening*

"I... heard rumors. But Donovan hadn't said anything directly to me."

Detective Ward: "If he had fired you, Serena, that would've left you in a difficult position, wouldn't it?"

Serena: *nodding slightly* "Yes, it would've. But I would've found another job. I didn't kill him, Detective. I couldn't have done that to him, even if things weren't perfect between us."

Jasper Gale:

Detective Ward: "Jasper, you and Donovan had a complicated relationship, didn't you?"

Jasper: *biting back his frustration* "Complicated is one way to put it. Donovan was supposed to be my mentor. Instead, he threw me under the bus when it suited him."

Detective Ward: "And you lost a lot because of him. Financially, professionally. That must've been hard to swallow."

Jasper: *tightening his fists* "It was. Donovan ruined me, Detective. But I'm not a killer. I wanted to rebuild my career, not end his life."

Detective Ward: "Still, you knew his routines, his habits. You would've known exactly how to get to him, especially with something as subtle as poison."

Jasper: *scoffing* "Knowing someone's habits doesn't make me a murderer. I hated the man, but I wasn't going to kill him. I wanted to beat him, to prove I didn't need him to succeed."

Elena Rhodes:

Detective Ward: "Elena, you and Donovan were seen arguing before his death. What was that about?"

Elena: *crossing her arms* "It was nothing. Just a stupid argument. We argued all the time, but it didn't mean anything."

Detective Ward: "Still, you've been with Donovan for a while now. It's no secret people questioned your motives. Did you argue about money?"

Elena: *sighing* "People always assume that. Yes, Donovan had money, but I wasn't with him for that. Our argument had nothing to do with it."

Detective Ward: "Then what was it about?"

Elena: *hesitating* "He was being controlling, as usual. I didn't like it, but that's just how he was. It didn't mean I wanted him dead."

OPTION 1: ACCUSE SCARLETT

Option 2: Accuse Noah
Option 3: Accuse Serena
Option 4: Accuse Jasper
Option 5: Accuse Elena

Whodunit "Live" Your Thoughts

This is where you can write your thoughts about who you think killed Donovan. You can do this before making your decision or after. There are plenty of moments throughout to make your choice.

Option 1: Accuse Scarlett

If you chose Scarlett Blakewell, you'd be wrong. Despite her anger and impending divorce, Scarlett was focused on financial revenge. She needed Donovan alive to secure her settlement.

Why Jasper?

- **Access:** As Donovan's former protégé, Jasper knew his routines well, including his favorite cocktail and where he would be throughout the night.

- **Motive:** The combination of professional sabotage and personal betrayal fueled Jasper's desire for revenge. Killing Donovan was, in Jasper's eyes, the only way to regain his dignity and rebuild his shattered reputation.

- **Behavior:** Jasper's simmering resentment was masked by his outward professionalism, but his hatred ran deeper than anyone realized.

- **Elena Rhodes:** While Elena was unhappy with Donovan, she had too much to lose by killing him. Her argument with Donovan was nothing more than frustration, not a murderous intent.

Option 2: Accuse Noah

If you chose Noah Hart, you'd be wrong. Noah was a fierce business rival, but his ambitions were too focused on beating Donovan in the market, not through murder.

Option 3: Accuse Serena

If you chose Serena Monroe, you'd be wrong. Serena's loyalty may have wavered, but her grief was genuine. She wanted to stay by Donovan's side, not eliminate him.

Option 4: Accuse Jasper

If you chose Jasper, you'd be correct! As Donovan's former protégé, Jasper knew his routines well, including his favorite cocktail and where he would be throughout the night. The combination of professional sabotage and personal betrayal fueled Jasper's desire for revenge. Killing Donovan was, in Jasper's eyes, the only way to regain his dignity and rebuild his shattered reputation. Jasper's simmering resentment was masked by his outward professionalism, but his hatred ran deeper than anyone realized.

Option 5: Accuse Elena

If you chose Elena Rhodes, you'd be wrong. While Elena was unhappy with Donovan, she had too much to lose by killing him. Her argument with Donovan was nothing more than frustration, not a murderous intent.

Whodunit "Live" Your Thoughts

This is where you can write your thoughts about who you think killed Donovan. You can do this before making your decision or after. There are plenty of moments throughout to make your choice.

About the Author

I have been wanting to write books for a while but never knew how. When writing a book, I always go with something random and don't always know what I want to write about. Sometimes there are a lot of different reasons for this, but for me personally, I just think of something random and go with it. There are times when I will use an AI to help me, but I was just messing around. I love how this book turned out and I hope you enjoy it.

Milton Keynes UK
Ingram Content Group UK Ltd.
UKHW020406021124
450424UK00014B/1454